RHINOS DON'T EAT PANCAKES

Anna Kemp & Sara Ogilvie

SIMON AND SCHUSTER

London   New York   Sydney

For Monty, with love – AK

*For Avril and Robert
(never too busy to listen)* – SO

SIMON AND SCHUSTER

First published in Great Britain in 2011 by Simon and Schuster UK Ltd
1st Floor, 222 Gray's Inn Road, London WC1X 8HB
A CBS Company

Text copyright © 2011 Anna Kemp
Illustrations copyright © 2011 Sara Ogilvie

The right of Anna Kemp and Sara Ogilvie to be identified as
the author and illustrator of this work has been asserted by them
in accordance with the Copyright, Designs and Patents Act, 1988

A CIP catalogue record for this book is available from the British Library upon request

ISBN: 978-1-84738-877-3 (HB)
ISBN: 978-1-84738-878-0 (PB)

Printed in China
1 3 5 7 9 10 8 6 4 2

Do you ever get the feeling that your mum and dad aren't listening to a word you say?
You do? Then you are just like Daisy. Her mum and dad never listen. Daisy could tell them that their hair was on fire or that the dog had eaten the postman but they would just nod and say, "That's nice dear," or "Tell your gran," or "Can't you see I'm on the phone?"

So when, one day, Daisy had something really important to say, guess what?
NOBODY LISTENED.

So this is what happened . . .

Daisy was eating her breakfast when a big purple rhino strolled into the kitchen.

That's right,
a big purple rhino!

It was as big as a bus and as purple as a plum.

It was also a bit peckish. So it took a chomp of Daisy's pancake and went upstairs.

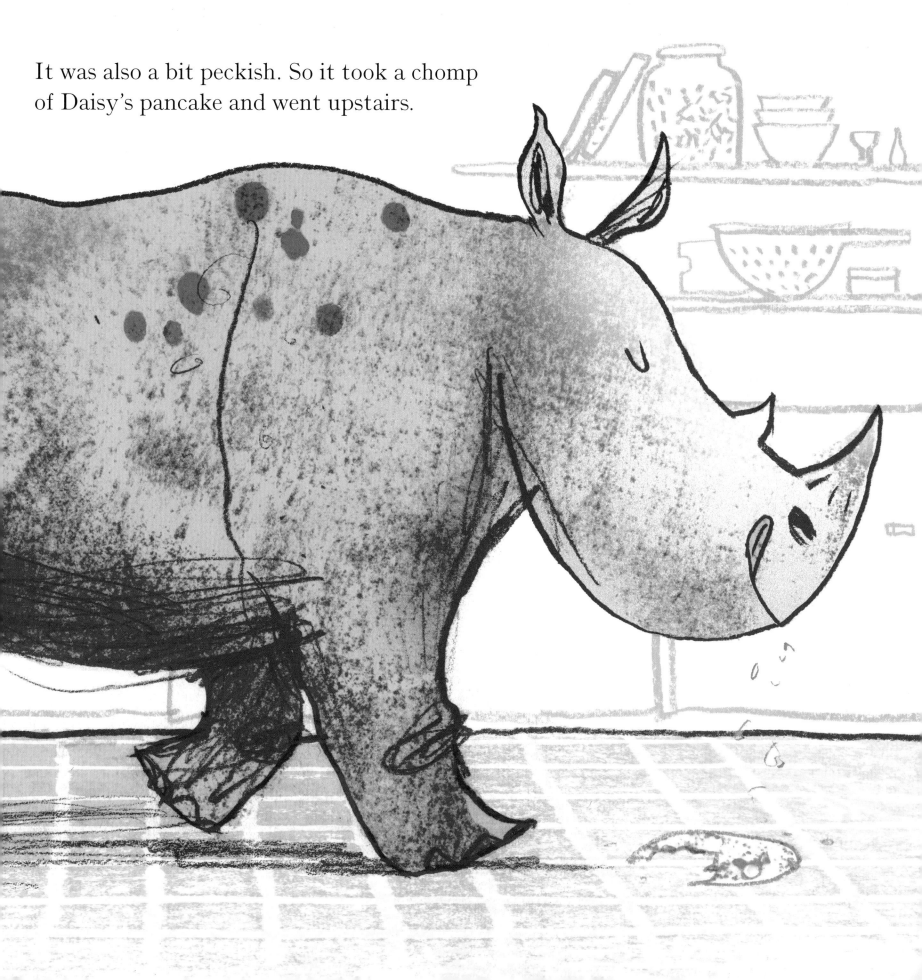

"Mum! Mum!" Daisy called.
"There's a big—"

"Tell your dad," said Mum.
"He'll catch it in a mug and throw it out of the window."

"Dad! Dad!" said Daisy.
"There's a big, there's a huge—"

"Shhh!" said Dad. "The spider can wait."

"It's not a spider!" Daisy shouted.
"It's a big, purple RHINOCEROS!"

But, as usual, **NOBODY LISTENED.**

Meanwhile, the rhino made himself right at home.

Daisy saw him in the hall,

and glimpsed him in the garden.

She spied him in the bathroom, and surprised him on the loo.

But every time she tried to tell her parents they'd say, "Shhhh! Daisy. Can't you see we're BUSY?"

Daisy's parents were busy all week.

So Daisy began to talk to the rhino instead.

Soon they became good friends.

They played hoop-la, and made pizza together,
and the rhino tickled Daisy until she thought she'd burst.
But Daisy's parents didn't notice.

Until the pancakes ran out.

"Who ate all the pancakes?"
yelled Dad looking straight at Daisy.

"It was the rhino," she said.

"Rhinos don't eat pancakes," said Dad.

"This one does!" cried Daisy. "I saw him in the kitchen."

"A rhino?" said Mum.

"In the kitchen?" said Dad.

"YES!" said Daisy. "Exactly!"

Mum and Dad roared with laughter.
    "Whatever next?" they hooted. "A shark in the toilet?
    A polar bear in the fridge?"

    "**THERE HE IS, LOOK!**" Daisy yelled.

But Mum and Dad were so busy laughing they didn't even notice.

"Come on, Rhino," said Daisy, "I've had enough of this."

The rhino tickled Daisy with his horn.
But she was far too glum to giggle.

"Mum and Dad never listen," she sighed. "They are
always a million miles away."
The rhino sighed deeply through his big purple nostrils.

"I'm sorry, Rhino," said Daisy. "Your family are a million miles away too, aren't they?"

The rhino nodded and a lilac tear rolled down his cheek.

Poor Rhino.

That night, Daisy sat up, thinking of ways to get the rhino back home to his family.

He was too heavy for a hot air balloon,

and too big for Daisy's rubber dinghy.

She thought about lending him her
bike, but the helmet would never fit.

The next morning, Mum and Dad had a surprise.
"We're taking you to the zoo!" said Mum. "So you can see
a REAL rhino."
"What do you think of that?" grinned Dad.

Daisy thought it was a stupid
idea when there was already
a perfectly good rhino sitting
on the sofa.

But she didn't say so.
What was the point?
NOBODY WOULD LISTEN.

At the zoo, Daisy saw yellow giraffes . . .

bright red parrots . . .

orange and black tigers, and grass green snakes.

But she couldn't help thinking about her poor purple rhino.
"Hurry up, Daisy," said Mum. "The rhinos are this way."

But what was this?

"Cripes!" gasped Mum.

"Well that explains the pancakes!" gasped Dad.

Mum, Dad and Daisy rushed back home
and guess what they saw when they got there . . .

That's right, the biggest,

purplest rhinoceros in town!

"What did I tell you?" Daisy said, grinning from ear to ear.

"I'm phoning the zoo," said Mum.

The rhino looked startled.

"No!" said Daisy. "Not the zoo. He needs to get back to his family. They are a million miles away."

"Well we'd better get a move on," said Dad. "The next flight to a Million Miles Away leaves this afternoon."

The rhino packed his suitcase while Daisy found his hat. Then they all pushed his big purple bottom into the back of the car . . .

and drove to the airport.

"I'll miss you," said Daisy as the rhino boarded the plane.
The rhino gave her a big purple hug. He would miss her too.

Back at home, Daisy began to feel lonely again.
Who would listen to her now?

But little did she realise that everything was about to change.

"Tell us about the rhino, Daisy," said Mum.
"Yes," said Dad. "Tell us about that big, purple, pancake-eating rhino."

So Daisy told them about the hoop-la and
the pizza and the tickles and guess what?

They listened and listened until she had completely run out of words.

IT WAS BRILLIANT.

"Is there anything else you'd like to tell us?"
asked Mum as she tucked Daisy into bed that night.

Daisy looked out onto the landing.

"No, that's all for now," said Daisy, smiling. "Night night!"

The pink polar bear would have to wait till tomorrow.